KT-422-047

Chris RIDDELL

Ottoline
and the
Purple Fox

MACMILLAN CHILDREN'S BOOKS

First published 2016 by Macmillan Children's Books

This edition published 2018 by Macmillan Children's Books
an imprint of Pan Macmillan
20 New Wharf Road, London N1 9RR
Associated companies throughout the world
www.panmacmillan.com

ISBN 978-1-5098-8155-0

Copyright © Chris Riddell 2016

The right of Chris Riddell to be identified as the author
and illustrator of this work has been asserted by him
in accordance with the Copyright, Designs and Patents Act 1988.

All rights reserved. No part of this publication may be reproduced,
stored in a retrieval system, or transmitted, in any form or by any means
(electronic, mechanical, photocopying, recording or otherwise),
without the prior written permission of the publisher.

135798642

A CIP catalogue record for this book is available from
the British Library.

Typeset by Nigel Hazle
Printed and bound by CPI Group (UK) Ltd, Croydon CR0 4YY

This book is sold subject to the condition that it shall not,
by way of trade or otherwise, be lent, resold, hired out,
or otherwise circulated without the publisher's prior consent
in any form of binding or cover other than that in which
it is published and without a similar condition including this
condition being imposed on the subsequent purchaser.

For Princess Joanna of Norfolk

Chapter One

Ottoline Brown lived in an apartment in the P. W. HUFFLEDINCK Tower, which looked like a pepper pot so everyone called it the Pepperpot Building.

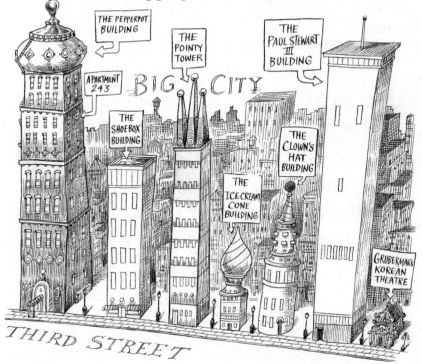

THE PEPPERPOT BUILDING

THE POINTY TOWER

THE PAUL STEWART III BUILDING

APARTMENT 243

BIG CITY

THE SHOE BOX BUILDING

THE CLOWN'S HAT BUILDING

THE ICE CREAM CONE BUILDING

GRUBERMAN'S KOREAN THEATRE

THIRD STREET

2

She lived with her best
friend, Mr. Munroe,
who was small and
hairy and came
from a bog in
Norway. Ottoline's
parents, Professor
and Professor Brown,
were Roving Collectors
and travelled the world collecting things
which they shipped home for Ottoline
to take care of. The collection was very
big, but Ottoline had lots of
help from all sorts of
people who came
to Apartment 243
every day.

OTTOLINE
ALWAYS
KEEPS A
NOTEBOOK
TO WRITE
DOWN
INTERESTING
THINGS AND
CLEVER
PLANS.

MR. MUNROE
LIKES TO
COLLECT
STRING.

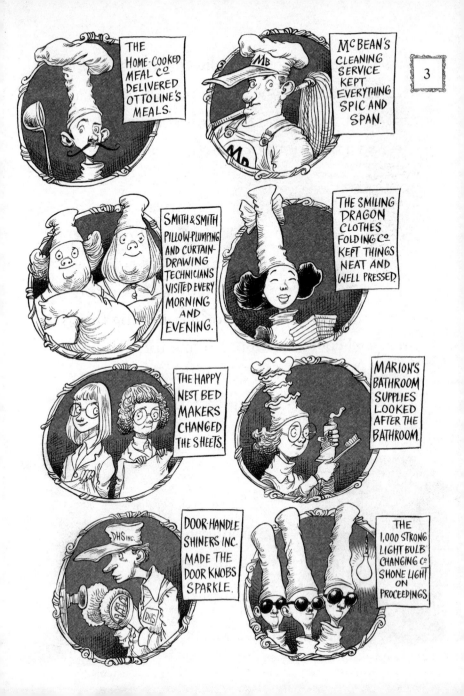

THE HOME-COOKED MEAL Co DELIVERED OTTOLINE'S MEALS.

MC BEAN'S CLEANING SERVICE KEPT EVERYTHING SPIC AND SPAN.

SMITH & SMITH PILLOW-PLUMPING AND CURTAIN-DRAWING TECHNICIANS VISITED EVERY MORNING AND EVENING.

THE SMILING DRAGON CLOTHES FOLDING Co KEPT THINGS NEAT AND WELL PRESSED.

THE HAPPY NEST BED MAKERS CHANGED THE SHEETS.

MARION'S BATHROOM SUPPLIES LOOKED AFTER THE BATHROOM.

DOOR-HANDLE SHINERS INC. MADE THE DOOR KNOBS SPARKLE.

THE 1,000 STRONG LIGHT BULB CHANGING Co SHONE LIGHT ON PROCEEDINGS.

As well as looking after the apartment and its collection, Ottoline and Mr. Munroe had all sorts of adventures together, like the time they foiled a notorious cat burglar . . .

YOU CAN READ ABOUT IT IN *OTTOLINE AND THE YELLOW CAT*

. . . and encountered the ghostly Horse of the Hammersteins . . .

YOU CAN READ ABOUT IT IN *OTTOLINE GOES TO SCHOOL*

. . . and visited the Abominable Troll of Trondheim, Quite Big Foot.

YOU CAN READ ABOUT IT IN *OTTOLINE AT SEA*

But whatever they did and wherever they went, Ottoline and Mr. Munroe looked out for each other, because they were best friends and had been for as long as Ottoline could remember.

MR. MUNROE LIKES HOT CHOCOLATE, SUNNY PLACES AND LENGTHS OF STRING. HE DOESN'T LIKE RAIN, HAVING HIS HAIR BRUSHED AND BEING MISTAKEN FOR A DOG.

OTTOLINE HAS ALWAYS LIKED PLAYING WITH AND BRUSHING MR. MUNROE'S HAIR.

THE BEIDERMEYER PIGEON-TOED OTTOMAN

6 Ottoline had decided to have a dinner party . . .

... and was out and about, planning for it in her notebook:

Guest list

Mrs. Pasternak ✓
and Morris

Cecily Forbes-Lawrence ✓
and Mumbles

Newton Knight and ✓
Skittles

The Sultana of
Pahang ✓
and Bye-Bye

The Bear in the
Basement?
↓

IGLOO
BOOT →

love the
Polar Bear Shoe Co.!

THE TALL TEACUP CAFE

THE POEM FROM THE LAMP POST

Dinner Party Menu

Porridge + Hot chocolate ✓

Super Douper soup ✓

Spaghetti Baguetti ✓

Sticky Biccy Pudding ✓

* Talk to The
Home Cooked
Meal co

← dogs
walking
past the cafe

Dinner Party Entertainment

Pin the tail on the balloon donkey ✗

Hide and Peek ✗

Pillow Island Hopping ✓

Truth or Stair ✓

Musical Bears ?

The Lamp-post Poem

note to myself

Ask the bear in the basement

Take a little bit of red
And a smudge or two of blue,
Mix them up together
To make the colour of you,
Velvet as the night in the silent streets,
Deep as the shadows as the city sleeps.

That evening at supper Ottoline noticed that
the dining-room lampshade collection was
getting a little cluttered. She could hardly
see Mr. Munroe at the other end of the table
because the double-fringed lamp muffler her
parents had shipped from Tibet was in the

THE
LAMP-POST
POEM

way. She knew he was having hot chocolate
and porridge though, because that was what he
always had.

"I think we need to de-clutter before our
dinner party," said Ottoline, taking a thoughtful
bite of her melted cheese and tomato crumpet.

14 After supper Ottoline went to the walk-in store closet in the hall. She turned the beautifully shined doorknob . . .

. . . and looked inside.

"This won't do at all,"
she told Mr. Munroe.
Mr. Munroe nodded.

Chapter Two

ROSIE RIVETER HEAD SCARF

LUMBER JACK SHIRT

SEVEN POCKET DUNGAREES

The next day Ottoline got up early and put on her "tidying-up" clothes. So did Mr. Munroe.

PERUVIAN LLAMA HERDER'S HAT

OTTOLINE'S STRIPY SOCKS

"Right," said Ottoline, "let's clear out the store closet and see what we've got."

Ottoline stood on tiptoe and reached up as far as she could. She took hold of the highest box.

Mr. Munroe took hold of the nearest box and pulled . . .

"Oh dear," said Ottoline. "Perhaps we could do with some help."

Just then the doorbell rang. Ottoline went to answer it while Mr. Munroe picked himself up and dusted himself off.

Ottoline opened the door. It was Pete and
Jackie from McBean's Cleaning Service.
 "How can we help?" said Pete with a smile.

Pete and Jackie helped Ottoline unpack the cardboard boxes and sort through everything. Ottoline's other helpers arrived and joined in.

Finally, when all the boxes had been opened, Ottoline decided what to do with the things inside . . .

MUSICAL PERFUME BOTTLES

DECORATIVE BOWLING BALLS

A CARVED UNICORN

INTERESTING THINGS WITH HOLES IN THE MIDDLE

CLOWN SKITTLES

WIND-UP THINGS

HELICOPTER HATS

SHEEP HORNS

COW BELLS

THESE ARE THE THINGS OTTOLINE KEPT.

DOG WHISTLES

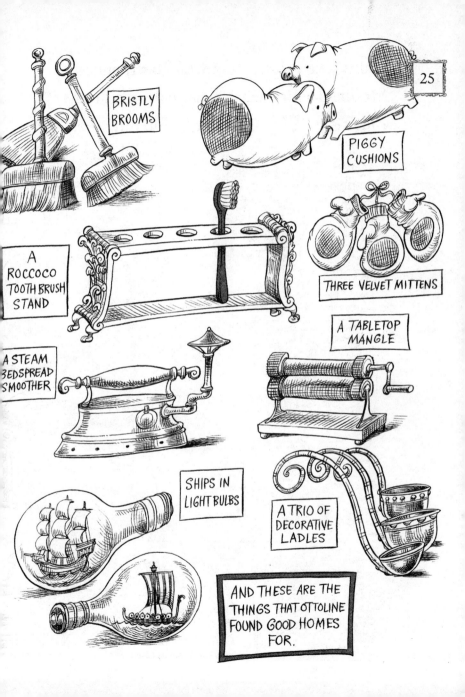

BRISTLY BROOMS

PIGGY CUSHIONS

A ROCCOCO TOOTH BRUSH STAND

THREE VELVET MITTENS

A TABLETOP MANGLE

A STEAM BEDSPREAD SMOOTHER

SHIPS IN LIGHT BULBS

A TRIO OF DECORATIVE LADLES

AND THESE ARE THE THINGS THAT OTTOLINE FOUND GOOD HOMES FOR.

Ottoline thanked
her helpers as they
left clutching their
cardboard boxes.

There were a few things left over.

"THIS WAY UP" STICKERS

BALL OF STRING

MYSTERIOUS OBJECTS

"You can have the string," Ottoline told
Mr. Munroe. "But the rest of it is junk."
Ottoline and Mr. Munroe packed the

junk in the box and took the elevator down to the lobby.

MR. SHAWCROSS AND MOLLY THE DUCK

MR. BEPE

EDWIN

BEATRICE AND SHOSHANA

THE LOBBY

NELLICENT WINSTANLEY AND BOOJUM

THE CRATTENSTONE-PUGHS.

In the lobby Ottoline saw someone she didn't recognize. The girl had fair hair and gloves that didn't match. She had a friend who was short and hairy and had extremely large feet. The girl reminded Ottoline of someone but she wasn't sure who.

"Her friend looks a little like you except with much bigger feet!" Ottoline laughed. Mr. Munroe didn't say anything. As Ottoline and Mr. Munroe watched, the girl and her friend left the Pepperpot Building and headed off towards Pettigrew Park and Ornamental Gardens.

"I wonder if they're going to Scoot 'n' Hoot," said Ottoline, clutching the cardboard box. Mr. Munroe tapped her on the shoulder with his umbrella.

"Yes, we can go there too," said Ottoline. "After we get rid of this junk."

Chapter Three

The alley next to the Pepperpot Building had a bin park where bins on wheels were all lined up in a row.

THERE WERE FOUR FOR EACH FLOOR OF THE PEPPERPOT BUILDING.

Ottoline was just about to take the lid off bin number thirty-four and put the junk inside when a furry face appeared.

It was a fox with purple fur.

"For me?" it said in a silky smooth voice. "How intriguing."

The Purple Fox took the cardboard box from Ottoline and looked inside.

"Why, this is perfect!" he exclaimed as he examined one of the "This Way Up" stickers. Then he paused. "But where are my manners? Do come inside."

"Inside?" said Ottoline uncertainly as the fox held out a paw.

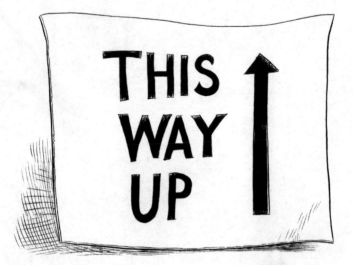

Ottoline took the Purple Fox's paw and climbed down inside bin thirty-four. Mr. Munroe followed her. The Purple Fox offered Ottoline a small swivel chair, then pulled up a tartan throw cushion and settled himself down.

"I like what you've done with the place," said Ottoline, looking around.

"Thank you," said the Purple Fox, adjusting his monocle. "Everything you see is recycled — it's amazing what people throw away. Take these stickers, for example. They're just what I've been looking for to wallpaper the extension."

"The extension?" asked Ottoline.

"Yes," said the Purple Fox, "I've just knocked through into number thirty-three."

"I had no idea anyone was living here," said Ottoline, impressed.

"Oh, you'd be surprised at the number of animals living right here in Big City," said the Purple Fox, "that no one ever notices."

The Purple Fox began taking the mysterious objects out of the box.

"Oh! These look very interesting!" he exclaimed, examining each one in turn.

"There are the turtles in Pettigrew Park, lapdogs in the Tall Teacup Cafe ," said Ottoline, "and Mr. Shawcross in my building has a pet duck . . ."

"I can show you far more interesting animals," said the Purple Fox smoothly. "In return for these lovely gifts, let me take you and your hairy friend on an Urban Safari."

"His name is Mr. Munroe," said Ottoline, "and we would love to!"

"Meet me on the corner at twelve o'clock tomorrow night," said the Purple Fox.

It was raining when Ottoline and Mr. Munroe
left the Purple Fox's den, so instead of going
to visit the park they headed to the cafe on
4th Street.

On 4th Street, Ottoline noticed that a new bookshop had opened up. She stopped and looked in the window. It had some of her favourite books on display . . .

. . . and one book she hadn't seen before.

They went inside.

"Hello, do you need any help?" said a voice.

Ottoline turned to see the girl from the lobby of the Pepperpot Building standing in front of her.

"I'd like to buy this book," said Ottoline, picking up the one she'd seen in the window.

"Excellent choice," said the girl. "I think you'll enjoy it. I like your hat, by the way."

"Thank you," said Ottoline. "I like your cardigan."

"My name's Ottoline Brown," said Ottoline. "You remind me of someone, but I can't think who."

"My name's Myrrh Treesister," said the girl, "and it's funny because you remind me of someone too . . ."

Ottoline bought the book with the money she kept in pocket number three.

"I don't suppose you'd like to pop over to the Tall Teacup Cafe and have a cup of tea with me?" asked Myrrh. "Miss Macintosh can look after the shop, can't you, Miss Macintosh?"

Miss Macintosh looked up from her knitting and nodded.

Mr. Munroe was fascinated by the ball of wool at her rather large feet.

"What a coincidence," said Ottoline. "Mr. Munroe and I were just on our way there, weren't we?"

But Mr. Munroe was too busy examining the ball of wool to answer.

At the Tall Teacup Cafe, Myrrh told Ottoline all about herself. Her parents, Doctor and Doctor Treesister, were Roving Book Collectors and had opened the 4th Street Bookshop because there was no room left in their apartment for their growing book collection. Myrrh lived in Apartment 342 of the Paul Stewart III Building, which everyone called the Paul Stewart III Building because it didn't look like anything else. Miss Macintosh lived with her. She was a small, hairy, big-footed person from a rocky island in the Baltic Sea.

"These crumpets are good," said Myrrh, "but not as good as the Home-Cooked Meal Company's."

"You know Jean-Pierre?" exclaimed Ottoline. "He's cooking for my dinner party. Would you and Miss Macintosh like to come?"

"We'd love to," said Myrrh. "But Miss Macintosh is a fussy eater."

"No problem at all," said Ottoline.

When Ottoline and Mr. Munroe got home they found a pile of letters waiting for them on the welcome mat.

ONE WAS A POSTCARD FROM HER PARENTS.

4ST BOOKS

WELCOME

After supper Ottoline settled down on the Beidermeyer armchair to open her mail.

Chapter Four

O ttoline read the postcard from her parents first. Although they weren't there, reading their postcards made Ottoline feel that they weren't so far away. She missed them very much.

MR. MUNROE HAS A HAIRBRUSH IN CASE OTTOLINE FEELS SAD. BRUSHING HIS HAIR ALWAYS MAKES HER FEEL BETTER.

THIS WAS ON THE BACK.

POSTCARD

WET WINDY
13 · 4 · 16
BALTIC

5c

Dearest O, These are saltwater selkies from Heligoland. The locals call them "the watchers on the rocks" because they like sea views. Found some interesting Baltic baubles which we'll ship home. Pa sends his best,

lots of love, Ma

S. The hall closet needs sorting out × × × ×

Miss O Brown,

Apt. 243

The Pepperpot Bld.

3rd Street,

BIG CITY 3001

THESE WERE THE OTHER
LETTERS OTTOLINE OPENED.

Marion's
— Bathroom supplies —
- SQUEEZING TUBES OF TOOTHPASTE FOR 25 YEARS -

Dear Miss Brown, The toothbrush
stand is beautiful! Thank you
so much,
Yours sincerely,
Marion Lloyd.

MB
McBEAN'S CLEANING
— SERVICE —
"you spill; we mop!"

Dear Miss Brown,
Big thankyou for
those brilliant brooms! They
have pride of place in our
show rooms on 5th street,
See you tomorrow,

Pete

Smith &
Smith
PILLOW-PLU
&
CURTAIN-DRAWING
TECHNICIANS
— WE LIVE TO PLUMP —

Love the
Pig cushions,
Kate + TERESA
♡

The Smiling Dragon
- ALL YOUR
FOLDING
NEEDS -
CLOTHES FOLDING

TABLETOP
MANGLE

Madame Wong

Happy Nest
BED MAKERS

Dear Miss Brown,
So kind of you to give us the steam bedspread smoother, it works like a DREAM!
Best wishes,
C and C.

— POLISHING IS MY LIFE
D.H.S.
DOOR HANDLE
SHINERS
INC.

A BIG THANK YOU
FROM
BIG DOUG.

☙ THE ☙
HOME COOKED MEAL Cₒ

Dearest Mademoiselle Ottoline,
— Your Menu —

Starter
Super dooper Soup

Main Course
Spaghetti baguetti

Dessert Sticky Biccy pudding

special orders —
Porridge and hot chocolate
Choco flakes and malted milk
Regards, Jean-Pierre

THE
1,000-STRONG
LIGHTBULB CHANGING Cₒ

Dear OB,
Cheers for the ships in Lightbulbs —
they're cool,
signed,

P.T.O.

"Thank you for letting me brush your hair, Mr. Munroe," said Ottoline. "I feel better now."

OTTOLINE SAVES ALL HER PARENTS' POSTCARDS AND KEEPS THEM IN HER POSTCARD COLLECTION.

Mr. Munroe handed Ottoline the book she'd bought from the 4th Street Bookshop.

They settled
down in the
Beidermeyer
armchair . . .

. . . and read
the whole book
from beginning
to end.

"I'd love to meet Ada Goth," said Ottoline
sleepily.

"Have you seen my stripy socks anywhere?" asked Ottoline the next morning. "I think I'll wear them on the Urban Safari tonight."

Mr. Munroe shook his head.

"I'll ask the bear in the basement," said Ottoline. The doorbell rang. "After breakfast, that is," she added.

MR. MUNROE HAD JUST BRUSHED OTTOLINE'S HAIR BECAUSE SHE ASKED HIM TO.

After breakfast Ottoline went down to the basement.

THE BEAR IN THE BASEMENT IS A GOOD FRIEND OF OTTOLINE'S AND PREFERS THE BASEMENT TO HIS COLD CAVE IN CANADA.

65

The bear hadn't seen Ottoline's stripy socks, but he did want her to meet his visitors.

Libby the polar bear and McNally the penguin from the Polar Bear Shoe Company were visiting Big City to show their latest shoe designs to the 3rd Street Shoe Store.

DUFFEL BAG OF SHOE SAMPLES

THE POLAR BEAR SHOE Co.

Ottoline was delighted to see them. The Polar
Bear Shoe Company made her favourite shoes
and she had lots of them in her Odd Shoe
collection.

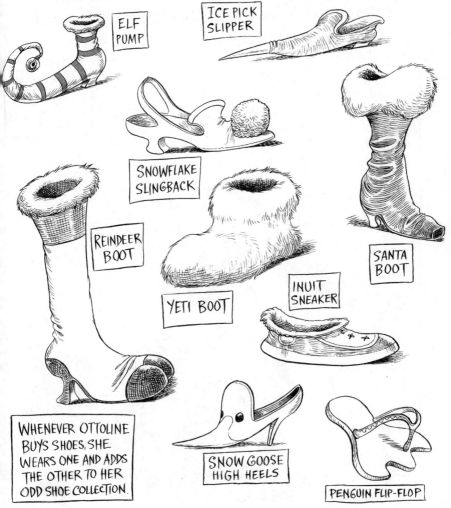

ELF PUMP

ICE PICK SLIPPER

SNOWFLAKE SLINGBACK

REINDEER BOOT

YETI BOOT

SANTA BOOT

INUIT SNEAKER

SNOW GOOSE HIGH HEELS

PENGUIN FLIP-FLOP

WHENEVER OTTOLINE BUYS SHOES, SHE WEARS ONE AND ADDS THE OTHER TO HER ODD SHOE COLLECTION.

After she had caught up on all the news from the Polar Bear Shoe Company, Ottoline listened to the pipes for a while. It's how she knew everything about everyone in the Pepperpot Building.

That night Ottoline and Mr. Munroe got dressed in their exploring clothes.

DOUBLE FASTENER CARRIAGE COAT

LARGE SHABBY RAINCOAT

MR. MUNROE REMEMBERED THAT HE HAD BORROWED OTTOLINE'S STRIPY SOCKS.

NEW SHOES

URBAN SOMBRERO

GOOSE HEAD UMBRELLA

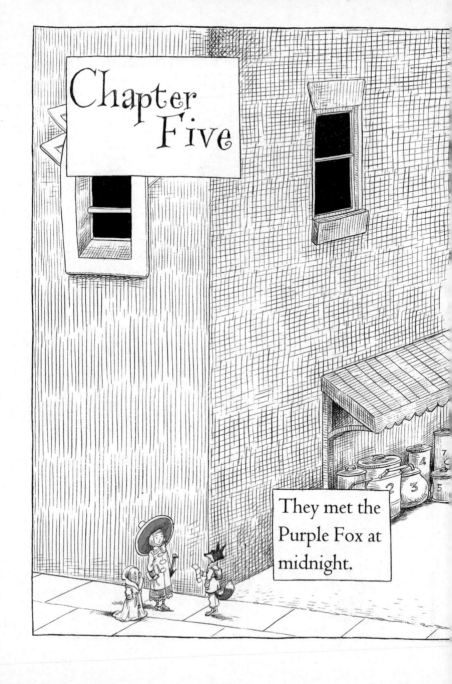

Chapter
Five

They met the
Purple Fox at
midnight.

73

The Purple Fox took them to the fire escape at the back of the Blitzenbilder Building that overlooked Big City Library.

74

A LAMP-POST POEM

YOU CAN READ IT ON PAGE 110.

As they watched, a flock of blue flamingos took off from their roosts on the roof of Big City Library and swooped down to land on the lamp posts in the piazza.

IF YOU WANT TO FIND OUT MORE ABOUT THE FLAMINGOS GO TO PAGE 108.

Next the Purple Fox took them to the roof of the muffin stand on 4th Street and Windmill.

A LAMP-POST POEM

YOU CAN RE IT ON PAGE

The manhole covers on 4th Street rose up and lots of small meerkats appeared.

IF YOU WANT TO FIND OUT MORE GO TO PAGE 112.

84

MAIL

LAMP-
POST
POEM

YOU CAN READ
IT ON PAGE 118.

Then the Purple Fox
took them to the
mailbox on 5th Street,
and they hid inside.

As they peeped out from the mailbox they saw a herd of miniature zebra trot along 5th Street and cross the road.

"And finally," said the Purple Fox smoothly,
"we come to the highlight of our Urban Safari.
Please step this way." A lady fox was standing
in an alleyway next to a basket and a winch.
She had a lovely red fur.

"Who's that?" asked Ottoline.

"Oh, that's just my assistant, the Crimson Vixen," said the Purple Fox as they stepped into the basket.

The Crimson Vixen turned the winch and the basket rose.

"Your assistant's fur is a very pretty colour," said Ottoline.

"Really?" said the Purple Fox. "I hadn't noticed."

The basket rose higher and higher until it came to the end of the rope.

"Now," whispered the Purple Fox, "we must stay very quiet and wait."

"Wait for what?" whispered Ottoline.

"You'll see," said the Purple Fox with a smile.

Chapter Six

They waited and waited but down below, in the garden on the roof of the 1st Street Fashion Store, nothing stirred.

"I think we might need these," said the Purple
Fox smoothly, taking the mysterious objects
Ottoline had given him from his haversack
and assembling them.

"It's a fishing rod!" exclaimed Ottoline.
"Who'd have thought?"

"It was missing its line," said the Purple
Fox. "But apart from that it's in excellent
condition."

"Mr. Munroe thought the line was string,"
said Ottoline.

Mr. Munroe didn't say anything.

Then the Purple Fox took a bunch of bananas
from under the seat and tied them to the
fishing line. He handed the fishing rod to
Ottoline.

"Try this," he said with a smile.

Ottoline lowered the bananas on the end of
the fishing line down towards the roof garden.
The moonlight glittered on the leaves of the
tropical plants and shrubs.

The Purple Fox, Ottoline and Mr. Munroe
waited . . .

... and waited ...

... until, all of a sudden, a large, hairy hand appeared. It stretched up out of the undergrowth and plucked a single banana from the bunch on the end of the fishing line.

More arms appeared, followed by heads.

They watched the gorillas dress up and parade through the rooftop jungle garden.

"I've had a wonderful time," said Ottoline, lowering the last of the bananas. "Mr. Munroe and I were just wondering if you and the Crimson Vixen would like to come to our dinner party."

"That sounds fascinating," said the Purple Fox smoothly.

Chapter Seven

When they got home Ottoline and Mr. Munroe went straight to bed.

The next morning Ottoline read the notes she had made in her notebook. Mr. Munroe read the poems he had collected from the lamp posts.

A blue
library
flamingo

The Purple
Fox says
the flamingos
do the same
thing every night
before they head
to the harbour
to eat blue shrimps
and seaweed.

They land
on the
lamp posts
and warm
their feet-
one foot
at a
time.

Warm →
glow

... and Mr. Munroe read the first poem.

Wingbeat, wingbeat,
Cold feet, cold feet.

Blue, blue flamingo
In the warm lamp glow

Coming down to land
Blue flamingo lamp stand

Wingbeat, wingbeat,
Warm feet, warm feet.

The Lamp-post poet

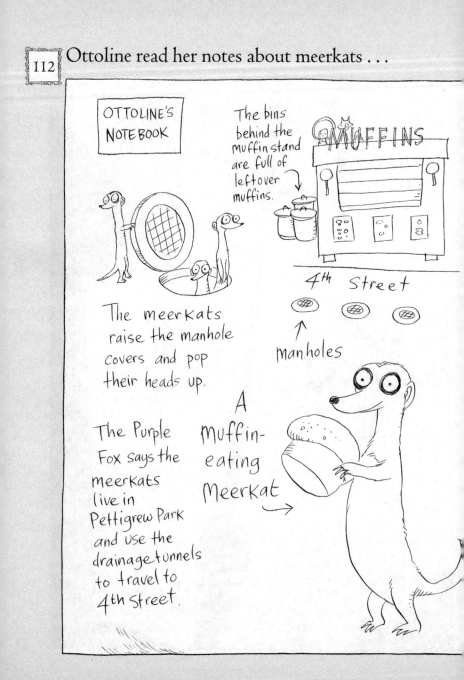

A tight squeeze!

Zebra crossing
↓

5th street

A miniature Zebra →

The Purple Fox says that the zebra herd lives in the Parking lot on 2nd street and they trot over to Pettigrew Park every night to graze.

Mr. Munroe read a poem about them.

Muffins are not the only cake.
But leftovers are free to take,
If twitchy paws and furry faces
Can seek out the cakey places.

Black and white, black and white,
In the middle of the night,
White and black, white and black,
Watch the Zebras trotting back.

The Lamp-post Poet

Ottoline read her notes about the shy gorillas . . .

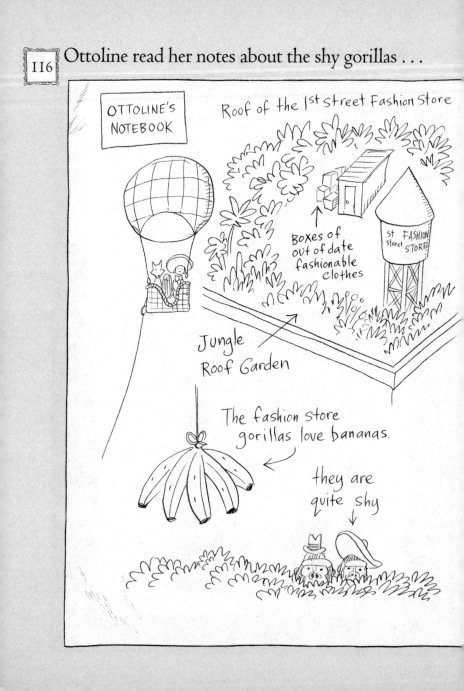

A fashion store gorilla

The Purple Fox says that the gorillas like bright colours and loud patterns, especially polka dots.

out of date trilby

out of date tartan shorts

Oh, Mr. Fox, Purple Fox,
So many things you see,
Oh, Mr. Fox, Purple Fox,
So many things but me.

Oh, Mr. Fox, Purple Fox,
So many places you go,
Oh, Mr. Fox, Purple Fox,
There's one thing you don't know.

Oh, Mr. Fox, Purple Fox,
I can't tell you though I try,
Oh, Mr. Fox, Purple Fox,
Because I am too shy.

The Lamp-post poet.

. . . that he found particularly interesting.

Chapter Eight

OTTOLINE WAS VERY GOOD IN THE PAPERFOLDING CLASS AT THE ALICE B. SMITH SCHOOL.

MR. MUNROE LIKED CUTTING OUT THE PAPER PEOPLE.

The next day Ottoline and Mr. Munroe made folded paper invitations and paper-people place settings for their dinner party.

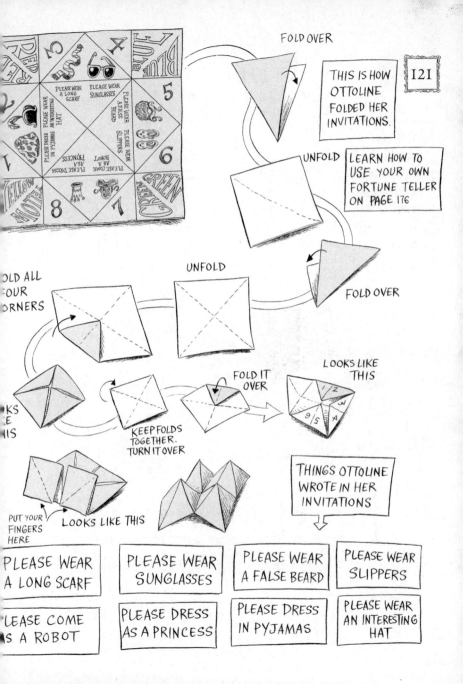

FOLD OVER

THIS IS HOW OTTOLINE FOLDED HER INVITATIONS.

121

UNFOLD

LEARN HOW TO USE YOUR OWN FORTUNE TELLER ON PAGE 176

FOLD OVER

FOLD ALL FOUR CORNERS

UNFOLD

LOOKS LIKE THIS

KEEP FOLDS TOGETHER. TURN IT OVER

FOLD IT OVER

LOOKS LIKE THIS

THINGS OTTOLINE WROTE IN HER INVITATIONS

PUT YOUR FINGERS HERE

LOOKS LIKE THIS

PLEASE WEAR A LONG SCARF

PLEASE WEAR SUNGLASSES

PLEASE WEAR A FALSE BEARD

PLEASE WEAR SLIPPERS

PLEASE COME AS A ROBOT

PLEASE DRESS AS A PRINCESS

PLEASE DRESS IN PYJAMAS

PLEASE WEAR AN INTERESTING HAT

McNALLY

LIBBY

THE BEAR

CECILY

MUMBLES

MORRIS

MRS. PASTERMAK

MISS MACINTOSH

MYRRH

NEWTON

SKITTLES

THE CRIMSON VIXEN

THE PURPLE FOX

THE SULTANA

BYE-BYE

OTTOLINE

MR. MUNROE

THESE WERE THE PAPER PEOPLE.

When they had finished, Ottoline gave the
invitations to Max the paper boy to deliver
to each of the guests personally. All, that
is, except the one for the bear and his
friends in the basement. Ottoline
delivered that one when
she went to do her
laundry.

INTERESTING KNITTED HAT

Myrrh and Miss Macintosh were almost the last to arrive.

"I like your pyjamas," said Ottoline.

Everybody chatted
until the dinner
gongs sounded.

"The Purple Fox is late," said Ottoline.

The first course was served by the Home-Cooked Meal Company.

ELECTRICITY

GRASS

CHOCO
FLAKES

A BANANA

OATS

PORRIDGE

"Delicious tomato soup," said Myrrh. "And
Miss Macintosh loves her Choco Flakes. It's
all she ever eats."

SPAGHETTI BAGUETTI

The second course
was served.

"Yummy pasta," said the bear, slurping a
strand of spaghetti into his mouth.

"There's no sign
of this Purple Fox of
yours," said Cecily.
"Are you sure you
didn't make him up,
Ottoline? I once had
a blue kangaroo as
an imaginary
friend."

CHOCOLATE-
COATED
BISCUITS

CARAMEL
SAUCE

STICKY BICCY PUDDING

Pudding
was served.

"This dessert
is divine,"
cooed Mrs.
Pasternak.

"You must give me the recipe."

After dinner, everyone went into the living
room for fun and games. They were just about
to begin when there was a tap-tap-tap at the
window.

It was the Purple Fox. The Crimson Vixen
held the window open and he stepped off the
fire escape and into the living room.

"I'm so sorry I'm late," he said, "but my
assistant was late opening my mail."

"She does look a little distracted," said
Ottoline.

"Does she?" said the Purple Fox. "I hadn't
noticed."

"Well, I never!" exclaimed the Purple Fox when Ottoline introduced him to Myrrh.

"You two could be sisters, you're so alike!"

"Now you mention it . . ." said Ottoline thoughtfully. "Now, who wants to play Pillow Island Hopping?"

PILLOW ISLAND HOPPING:
JUMP FROM PILLOW TO PILLOW
WITHOUT TOUCHING THE FLOOR.

The Purple Fox was
very good at jumping from
pillow to pillow but gallantly allowed Cecily
to win.

Then they played Truth or Stair, and the
Purple Fox told them about the most
embarrassing thing that had ever happened to
him and everyone laughed because he told the
story so well.

...WHAT I DIDN'T REALIZE UNTIL THE NEXT MORNING WAS MY NEW BIN BELONGED TO "MURRAY'S GOULASH SHACK"...

TRUTH OR STAIR: TELL A TRUE STORY OR CLIMB THE STAIRS.

When it was her turn, the Crimson Vixen chose to climb the stairs to the roof instead.

Mr. Munroe and Miss Macintosh went with her to keep her company.

They were gone for quite a long time.

MUSICAL BEARS:
A BEAR PICKS YOU UP
AND DANCES TILL
THE MUSIC STOPS.

When
they got
back from
the roof the
others were
just finishing a game of Musical Bears.

"Is that the time?" said Cecily. "I really must
be going. Mumbles and I have got carriage
croquet in the morning. It's been a lovely
evening."

The Crimson Vixen shook Ottoline's hand
and then shook Mr. Munroe's.

"Thank you for inviting me," she said shyly.

After the guests had left, Mr. Munroe showed Ottoline the rest of lamp-post poems he had collected.

Ottoline asked if she could brush Mr. Munroe's hair. It helped her think, especially when she had plans to make and tricky puzzles to solve.

When she had finished brushing, Ottoline began to plait Mr. Munroe's hair.

"I think we should try to help the lamp-post poet," she said thoughtfully. "And I'm working on a plan . . ."

Chapter Nine

The next day
Ottoline and
Mr. Munroe got up
early and went out.

They visited a
wooden crate in
the alley behind the Paul Stewart III Building
that Mr. Munroe had been told about the
night before.

The Crimson Vixen was surprised to see them.

"Mr. Munroe saw that you were unhappy last night," Ottoline told her, "so we're going to try to help."

"It's no good," said the Crimson Vixen. "The Purple Fox is so clever and talented and witty, but he just doesn't notice me and I'm too shy to tell him how I feel."

"Well," said Ottoline, "we need to show him how clever and talented *you* are. Mr. Munroe and I are already working on a clever plan, aren't we, Mr. Munroe?"

Mr. Munroe nodded and handed the Crimson Vixen his raincoat.

"Put this on and come with us," said Ottoline. We've got lots of friends who can help!"

First they visited the 4th Street Bookshop.

Then they had lunch in the Tall Teacup Cafe.

Next they visited Pettigrew Park and
Ornamental Gardens . . .

. . . and when they got home, Ottoline and Mr.
Munroe went down to the basement.

The plan was coming along nicely.

PAGES FROM OTTOLINE'S NOTEBOOK
pod
peas
look exactly alike
Two peas in a pod song.
LAMP-POST POEMS
Slim volume of poetry
hand made by the 4th street book shop.
lovely poems
fairy lights
from the 1,000 strong Lightbulb Changing Co
patchwork squares
selected by the Happy Dragon Clothes Folding Co
Recycled from out of date fashionable Clothes
Patchwork dress
stitched by 1st street Fashion Store Gorillas.

Shower
Curtains
from
Marion's
Bathroom
Supplies ☑

Put up by Smith and Smith
Pillow-Plumping and Curtain-
Drawing technicians ☑

Dress designs by Libby
the
Polar
bear ☑

149

← Polka
dots

← Tartan

☑

Sparkly
stars

FOLLOW
ME ← Recycled
"This Way
Up"
Sticker

Newton Knight's
Robo-copter.

☑

150 A week later, The Purple Fox heard a knock. When he opened the lid of his bin, he found a note, and saw Newton Knight's Robo-copter waiting for him patiently.

Chapter Ten

The Purple Fox arrived at the roof gardens of the 1st Street Fashion Store.

"Hello," said Ottoline. "I'm so pleased to see you."

"Please, step this way," said Myrrh.

"Just follow us," said Cecily and the Sultana together.

DRESSES
DESIGNED
BY LIBBY
THE POLAR
BEAR

Mr. Munroe and Miss Macintosh were
waiting beside a large pair of curtains.

First Cecily and
Mumbles performed
an interpretative
dance.

Then the Sultana and Bye-Bye juggled
coconuts . . .

... followed by Ottoline and Myrrh singing a song.

"And now . . ." said Ottoline, "introducing the very clever and extremely talented lamp-post poet, the Crimson Vixen!"

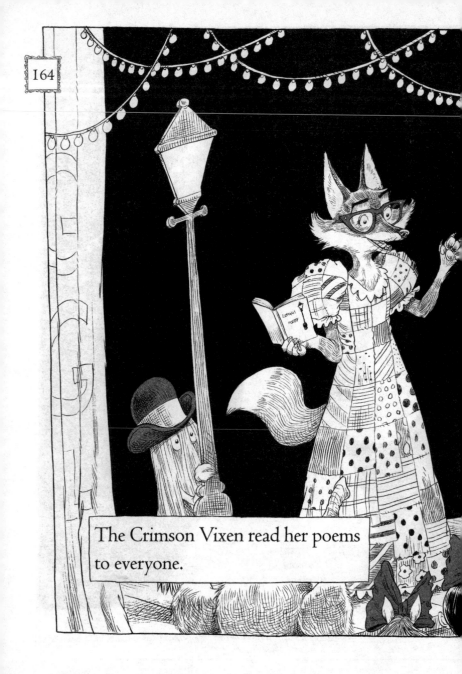

The Crimson Vixen read her poems to everyone.

"Why, Miss Crimson Vixen, I hadn't noticed how clever and talented you are," said the Purple Fox. "Until now."

"Please call me Magenta," said the Crimson Vixen shyly.

"You can call me Peregrine," said the Purple
Fox with a smile. "I've never noticed before
what a beautiful colour your fur is."

Magenta smiled.

"Would you like to dance?" asked the Purple Fox.

"I'd love to, Peregrine," she said.

The Purple Fox and the Crimson Vixen danced the foxtrot as the shy gorillas began to emerge from the jungle roof garden.

The party went
on all night.

As the sun rose, the Purple Fox and the
Crimson Vixen slipped away from the party
and, untying the rope, they waved as the
balloon sailed up into the early-morning sky.

"It's nice making new friends," said Ottoline sleepily. "But you, Mr. Munroe, will always be my BEST friend."

Mr. Munroe didn't say anything . . .

. . . but Ottoline felt a little squeeze on her hand.

Meet Ottoline Brown and her
best friend, Mr. Munroe.
No puzzle is ever too tricky
for the two of them to solve . . .

A string of daring burglaries have taken place
in Big City and precious pet dogs are disappearing
all over town. Can Ottoline and Mr. Munroe
come up with a clever plan to catch the robbers?

Ottoline Brown and her
best friend, Mr. Munroe,
are starting school . . .

. . . but they're not scared — even if it is haunted!
Ottoline is off to the Alice B. Smith School for the
Differently Gifted, but she is rather worried that
she doesn't have a special gift. Mr. Munroe is more
worried about the ghost who is said to haunt the
school halls at night. Does Ottoline discover her
hidden talent and can they expose the spook?

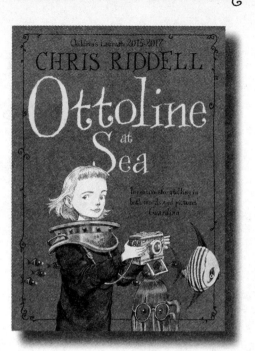

Ottoline Brown and her best
friend, Mr. Munroe, are
usually inseparable . . .

But Mr. Munroe has gone on a secret mission to
Norway to find the snaggle-toothed, super-hairy
Quite Big Foot. Ottoline sets off over the sea
by submarine, silver seaplane and even a raft to
find Mr. Munroe — before he comes face to face
with the terrible troll all on his own.

How to Use Your Fancy-Dress Fortune Teller

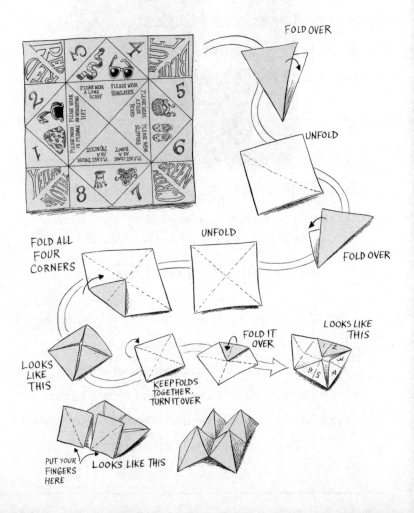

1. Put the thumb and forefinger of each hand into the fortune teller so that you can move the four corners.

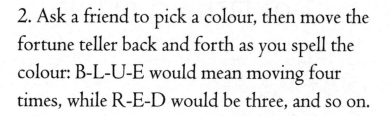

2. Ask a friend to pick a colour, then move the fortune teller back and forth as you spell the colour: B-L-U-E would mean moving four times, while R-E-D would be three, and so on.

3. Next, ask your friend to pick one of the numbers now visible on the inside of the fortune teller and then move it back and forth again as you count up to the number they've chosen.

4. It's time to pick a fortune! Your friend must pick one of the numbers on the inside of the fortune teller. Lift the flap to reveal their fancy-dress costume!

THINGS OTTOLINE WROTE IN HER INVITATIONS

PLEASE WEAR A LONG SCARF

PLEASE WEAR SUNGLASSES

PLEASE WEAR A FALSE BEARD

PLEASE WEAR SLIPPERS

PLEASE COME AS A ROBOT

PLEASE DRESS AS A PRINCESS

PLEASE DRESS IN PYJAMAS

PLEASE WEAR AN INTERESTING HAT

Cut out and colour in!